FOOTBALL FACTOR

FIRST MATCH

Alan Durant and Andrew Chiu

WAYLAND

www.waylandbooks.co.uk

"Well done," said the manager.

He shook Danny's hand.

"Thanks," said Danny.

4

FOOTBALL FACTOR

FIRST MATCH

First published in 2013 by Wayland

Text copyright © Alan Durant 2013
Illustrations © Wayland 2013

Wayland
338 Euston Road
London NW1 3BH

Wayland Australia
Level 17/207 Kent Street
Sydney, NSW 2000

Series Editor: Victoria Brooker
Series design: Robert Walster and Basement68
Cover design: Lisa Peacock
Consultant: Dee Reid

A CIP catalogue record for this book is available
from the British Library.
Dewey number: 823.9'2-dc23

ISBN 978 0 7502 7980 2

2 4 6 8 10 9 7 5 3 1

Printed in China

Wayland is a division of Hachette Children's Books,
an Hachette UK Company
www.hachette.co.uk

Danny looked at the team sheet.
There was his name! He was amazed.
He was playing on the wing for
Sheldon Rovers.

Danny was seventeen.

He had played in the reserves.

Now he was in the first team!

He was playing in the first round of
the Cup!

Danny couldn't sleep on
Friday night. He was so excited.
He couldn't wait for the game.

On Saturday the nerves kicked in.
Danny's legs were shaking.
He felt sick.

He kept going to the loo.
The other players laughed.

The players were in the tunnel
waiting. Kyle, the Team Captain,
was next to him.

"Good luck," he said. "Enjoy
your first match."

They went out on the pitch.

The crowd clapped and shouted.

Danny's heart pumped.

He ran to his place.

The game kicked off.

Danny's first pass wasn't good.

The ball rolled off the pitch.

The crowd groaned.

Danny's next pass was better.

He flicked the ball to Kyle.

Then he sprinted into space.

"Well played," said Kyle.

It was a hard first half. Danny went
back more than he went forward.
He had to defend a lot.

The opposing fullback was fast.
He liked to attack.

Sheldon went one down.
It was partly Danny's fault.
The fullback beat him and
crossed to the striker.

The striker scored.

At half-time it was 1-0.

"Come on, Danny," the manager
said. "I want that fullback to defend!"

Sheldon started the second half well.

They made some chances.

They forced some corners.

Danny saw more of the ball.

He ran at the fullback.

He got some crosses into the box.

Sheldon's striker, Naz, hit the bar.

The fullback started a counter attack.
He ran up the pitch.

Danny chased him.

He slid in and won the ball.

Now Danny was away.

The pitch was clear before him.

He sprinted and weaved.

He cut the ball back to Naz.

Thump!

The ball crashed into the net.

Sheldon were level, 1-1!

Danny was on fire now.

The fullback couldn't stop him.

Danny crossed the ball.

Naz headed a second goal.

The final whistle blew.

Sheldon had won 2 -1.

They were in the next round.

"Well played," said Kyle.
"Not bad for a first match,"
said the manager.

Danny couldn't stop grinning.
It had been a dream match!
He couldn't wait for the next game.

Read more stories about Sheldon Rovers.

Sheldon Rovers have made it to the Cup final. It is their manager Dave Brown's last match. Will Danny, Robby, Naz, Ledley and Tom play their best? Can they make Dave's day and win the Cup?

Danny is playing his first match for Sheldon Rovers. It is the first round of the Cup. He needs to play well to keep his place. But will nerves get the better of him?

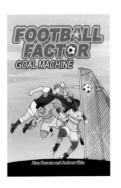

Naz is Sheldon Rover's top scorer. He is a goal machine. But suddenly things start to go wrong. He can't score at all. He loses his place in the team. Will he ever get his goal touch back?

Tom plays in goal for Sheldon Rovers. He has a lucky horseshoe that he takes to every match. But on Cup semi-final day it goes missing. Things start to go wrong. Has Tom's luck run out?

Robby keeps getting sent off. Now he has got a three-match ban and he feels down. Can he learn to control his temper? Will he ever get back in the team?

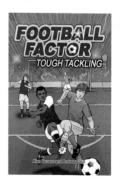

Ledley is a defender for Sheldon Rovers. He has been out injured for months. His first game is the Cup quarter final. Will he last the game? Will his tackling be strong enough?

FOR TEACHERS

About Freestylers

Freestylers is a series of carefully levelled stories, especially geared for struggling readers of both sexes. With very low reading age and high interest age, these books are humorous, fun, up-to-the-minute and edgy. Core characters provide familiarity in all of the stories, build confidence and ease pupils from one story through to the next, accelerating reading progress.

Freestylers can be used for both guided and independent reading. To make the most of the books you can:

- Focus on making each reading session successful. Talk about the text before the pupil starts reading. Introduce the characters, the storyline and any unfamiliar vocabulary.

- Encourage the pupil to talk about the book during reading and after reading. How would they have felt if they were one of the characters playing for Sheldon Rovers? How would they have dealt with the situations that the players found themselves in?

- Talk about which parts of the story they like best and why.

For guidance, this story has been approximately measured to:

National Curriculum Level: 1B
Reading Age: 6
Book Band: Orange

ATOS: 1.5
Lexile ® Measure [confirmed]: 140L